AMONG
STRANGLING
ROOTS

Among Strangling Roots

DARK FOLKLORE

Georgina Jeffery

Coblyn Press

First published by Coblyn Press 2022

Copyright © 2022 by Georgina Jeffery

This novel is entirely a work of fiction. The names, characters and incidents portrayed in it are the work of the author's imagination. Any resemblance to actual persons, living or dead, events or localities is entirely coincidental.

Georgina Jeffery asserts the moral right to be identified as the author of this work.

Cover designed by GetCovers

First edition

ISBN: 978-1-8381498-7-1

georginajeffery.com

Content Warning

Please be advised, this story contains reference to child abuse, mental illness, postnatal depression, and substance abuse.

The sky hung low and dark over the fields of Yellow Ridge Farm. Marion stared through thin window panes at the approaching rain clouds, where they dragged a grey veil over the distant hills.

Subdued conversation filled the rooms of her mother's house. The occasional clink of china betrayed a courageous individual confronting the buffet, where dainty sandwiches and vol-au-vents were picked at with little enthusiasm. A large Zuckerkuchen funeral cake took up the centre of the antique dining table.

Marion knew most of the hushed words were about her.

'Do you think she'll move in?'

'She works in the city, doesn't she? I heard she wanted to get as far away from here as possible ...'

'The farm's too run down to sell, the market is poor ...'

'It would be such a lovely family home. So much space for Lilli to run around in.'

'It could be just what they need. You know, a fresh start.'

Lilli sat on a stool in the corner, playing silently with one of her grandmother's rag dolls. The adults in the room showered her with doleful glances. *Poor thing,* they said. *She looks so sad.*

Marion rolled her eyes. Lilli wasn't sad. She barely knew her grandmother. This was just a free excuse to skip school. Her quiet, introspective play was a normal part of her personality; she wasn't given to running and whooping and screeching like other children.

Other children might get a lot out of living on a farm. The endless rolling fields could be a fantastical playground for a more audacious eight-year-old. They were the kind of fields you could spend all summer in. Marion certainly had.

Memories pricked insistently at her brain. There was a time when she would crawl through golden labyrinths of wheat for hours on end. Spend long evenings chewing on a straw of barley, instead of going home for dinner. Hunker in silence between stalks of green rye, while her mother stamped through the fields with a belt in her hand.

The fields beyond the window were touched with the first flushes of gold. The air was heavy, cloying. It looked set to be a muggy summer, full of thunderstorms and wet heat. A nightmare for planning harvest time, and potentially catastrophic for the quality of the grains.

Good, Marion thought. *Let's hope it all rots.*

Was the field in front of her barley, or wheat? She couldn't tell from this distance. A speck of something caught her eye, and she squinted through the glass. In the middle of the long field a figure moved, wading through the green and gold stalks. It was obscured by too much shadow to make out features, but it wore a wide-brimmed hat. Rather like the one her mother used to wear.

A hand touched her shoulder. Marion didn't flinch, but she did tense at the prospect of more idle small talk with strangers.

She turned around, affecting a polite tone. 'Yes?'

It was her mother's neighbour. Ingrid? That sounded right. She was a wizened raisin of a woman, all wrinkles and sun-blotched skin. She squeezed Marion's shoulder – an unwelcome gesture.

'Such a lot to manage, dear,' Ingrid said kindly, nodding to the fields. 'Especially for someone so young. Such a shame to lose your mother at an early age. Do let us know if you need help?'

Marion gave her a perfunctory smile. 'Thanks. We'll be fine.'

'I can give a good word for Walter, if you're looking for someone to manage the farm going forward. Worked with your mother for over twenty years, he has . . .'

'I will be selling the farm,' Marion said firmly. She allowed herself some pleasure in Ingrid's stunned expression. 'A few real estate companies have already approached me with offers.'

It didn't matter that it was a lie. What mattered was that they knew who made the decisions here. Oh, was that a flash of anger on Ingrid's face?

'But you can't–' Ingrid caught the comment before it fully left her mouth. She shut it tightly, jaw clenched.

I dare you, Marion said with her stare. *Tell me what to do with my own house.*

Ingrid backed down. 'Well. I hope it all goes well for you,' she replied in clipped tones.

She returned to the gaggle of other lean, sun-bleached women who had clearly been at the centre of her mother's social circle. A coven of old witches, the lot of them. Marion watched the news disperse among their troupe, and stared down every shocked glance fired in her direction.

That's right, she thought, sipping at her glass of wine. *I'm going to tear this place down. I'm going to tear it all down.*

She turned back to the window and the empty fields. In the corner, Lilli pulled the head off her ragdoll. Marion thought nothing of it.

* * *

The following week dragged by. Living out of suitcases, Marion took up residence in the house while she packed it up.

The place grated on her every nerve.

It was the kind of house that creaked in even the lightest of winds. Shoddily built, yet an enduring monument to her mother's vanities. Back when traditional values and traditional houses had turned popular again, and anyone with the bones of even a marginally old house could suddenly chase local esteem by renovating it.

Her mother took to the idea with enthusiasm. Despite an architect's best efforts, its fake timber-frame and red-brick façade made a mere mockery of a traditional Low German farmhouse. The high and steeply slanted gable roof had become an eyesore long ago, during Marion's childhood, when her mother had run out of money for proper thatch. She'd replaced it with cheap tiles that dropped off in the wind.

Marion had witnessed the original gutting of its insides, as well. The shrinking and expansion of rooms. The backwards replacement of modern amenities. Taps exchanged for antique models that leaked; modern plumbing ripped out in favour of old copper pipes.

She felt no nostalgia for it. No connection to the place as a home. It was just a house where she had lived.

And now it was a house she could not sell. Nobody wanted a fake, a poorly concealed counterfeit with crumbling foundations and faulty wiring.

Lights blinked on and off at random intervals as Marion moved through the house, taking stock of its contents. She had left Lilli curled up in an armchair in the front room, where she watched inane cartoons on a tablet. The girl spent most of her time in front of the screen. She wasn't the type of child to be interested in her surroundings. And she couldn't be trusted to help pack things into the right boxes, anyway.

So, it was all down to Marion to sort through the ramshackle clutter of her mother's life, and somehow determine what was worth selling and what was not. She strongly felt that a good deal of it *was not.*

But money was tight, and if she really *didn't* want to be forced into living in this house for good, then she had to find a way to pay the next month's rent on her home back in Hamburg.

'Stupid,' she muttered under her breath, for the hundredth time. So stupid to have taken that apartment. But when Karl walked out she'd been convinced she needed to find somewhere new. Somewhere to start again.

Marion glared into the cardboard box at her feet. So far, it was filled with cutlery. So *much* cutlery excavated from her mother's drawers. Why did one woman need so many sets of knives and forks and spoons? They were just another farce.

Marion dropped a handful of copper kitchen utensils on top. They landed with a teeth-grinding *clash* of metal.

They hadn't been a big family. For most of Marion's life it had been only her and her mother. Dad died when she was little, before the house had swapped its insides. She didn't remember ever getting all this cutlery out at once. Or the ugly green china, or the reams of white pressed cloth napkins.

Except after the funeral, she decided. Probably the only time most of it had seen any use at all.

She kicked the box away, already sick of looking at it. Her heels clacked on the cold hardwood floor as she paced a circuit round the large dining room. The enormous walnut sideboard was finally empty of its useless tableware; now rendered useless itself.

Marion tutted at it. It was a horrible thing, out of fashion in every respect. No doubt her mother had bought it for that very reason – as an *historic* item. It wasn't intended to be attractive, from the dull, dark hue of the timber to the knobbly carving that adorned it: a jumble of vines and leaves and berries and, on each of the three cupboard doors, a carved face poking out of the foliage.

Grotesque faces, too. Their eyes were pupilless, blank, but the mouths stretched open in grimaces. One leered at the viewer, upper lip curled in revulsion. The middle face bore a furious snarl, eyebrows meeting in the middle. The final expression was one of open fear. Its mouth gaped open in a silent scream as leaves encroached upon it.

Marion hated all of them.

No chance, she supposed, of rubbing the thing down and upcycling it with a 'vintage' makeover. Not even pretty pastel colours could hide those ghastly faces. And the thing was notched all over with age and wear.

She ran a finger along one edge.

'*Ow!*'

Marion yanked her hand back and sucked at the finger. A red drop of blood bloomed on her skin.

'Bastard thing.' She glared down at the splinter responsible and aimed a kick at the doors.

Her mother's voice loomed in her mind. *Don't you dare kick that!*

But Mum, it growled at me!

It did no such thing.

It did–

Marion's face turned with the memory of the slap. She touched her cheek.

Stupid girl! Why do I keep you? I shall have you off to the Rye Aunt if you tell lies again!

Marion's lips pursed. Ah yes, the Rye Aunt. That ever-present bogeyman her mother had relied on to back up discipline in a fatherless household.

Be good, else the Rye Aunt shall swap you with a changeling child, and no one will know you've disappeared. The changeling shall wear your clothes and eat your food, all while the Rye Aunt makes you suck hot tar from her breasts and locks you inside her iron butter churn. If you misbehave she will pound you into butter. So, be good. There is no other option but to be good.

Marion suppressed a shudder. The house was full of draughts. She pulled down her messy bun of hair and compulsively retied it, screwing it tightly to the top of her head.

She'd toss the sideboard out on the drive, she decided. Maybe find a freecycle group online to collect it. It could be someone else's problem.

Marion grabbed one end of the bulky cupboard and heaved. She grunted as painful pressure weighed down her spine. The sideboard dragged an inch, with an unearthly screech across the floor.

Marion let go, puffing for air. The damn thing was too heavy. She'd need help.

'Lilli!' She pivoted and strode out to the hall.

The girl was nowhere to be seen. Marion frowned at the empty living room, where pink paisley armchairs and fluted glass ornaments were the only remaining features. And also Lilli's tablet, left abandoned on the cracked windowsill.

Marion picked it up. Her pinched lips reflected from the screen, along with a garish hedgehog cartoon, still playing. She switched it off and glanced up to the window.

Lilli was in the field in front of the house. She was talking to someone.

Marion jerked forward, left hand slapping against the glass. In the middle of the cornfield, Lilli craned her neck up to a tall figure, obscured under the darkness of a wide-brimmed hat.

Who could that possibly be? Not Ingrid. Too tall. Too gangly. Male? Something in the silhouette said female. Marion squinted, searching for features. The stranger placed a hand on Lilli's shoulder; Marion's stomach curdled.

She rushed onto the front porch, stamped down the wide gravel path. 'Lilli!' she shouted, expecting the girl to turn as soon as she heard her name.

But Lilli remained stock still, staring into whatever eyes lay beneath the broad hat.

'*Lilli!*' Marion called again, this time with an insistent tinge of anger. Could the girl not hear her? She couldn't be more than fifty metres away. What the *hell* was the stranger telling her?

Thrumming with outrage, Marion stepped across the field boundary into the chest-high rows of wheat. 'You *listen* to me, young lady! Turn around!'

She marched forward, heels sinking unevenly into the soft soil. Scratchy spikelets of wheat whipped at her arms. She batted them away, wading as if swimming, suddenly unable to find the path between the ploughed rows. Lilli was just ahead, yet somehow further than she was before.

The tall figure half-turned in Marion's direction.

The sun was high. That must be why there was only shadow beneath the hat. But it was such a distinctive hat.

A glint of metal in its brim caught the light.

Squirming nausea crawled up Marion's spine as she recognised the blue butterfly hatpin that her mother had always worn.

'Who are you?' she asked, but the words rang weirdly in her ears as though they'd come from a great distance.

She pumped her legs harder, fighting to catch up to them. The stranger turned back to Lilli, stooped as if to kiss her. Marion stretched out a hand–

'*Lilli!*'

She clamped down on Lilli's shoulder, stared into a shocked white face.

'What are you doing?' Marion demanded. She

looked up to gouge out an answer from the shadowed figure, but it had disappeared.

She stared mutely at the empty patch of field. Empty in every direction. Wheat stalks rustled in mockery all around her. 'What . . . ?'

Her grip tightened on Lilli's shoulder. The girl winced away in pain – Marion yanked her back. 'Who were you talking to? Answer me. Who was in this field with you? *I saw you.*'

Lilli mumbled something incomprehensible.

Marion shook her. '*Stupid girl.* You know better than to talk to strangers! Do you know how worried I was? Stupid. Do you hear me? *Stupid!*'

She released her hold, noting the sullen expression that flashed across her daughter's face.

'Don't pull that face at me. Get inside,' Marion snapped. 'Else I'll tell the Rye Aunt to take you away. Then you'll be sorry.'

It just slipped out. The Rye Aunt. Like she'd always been just on the tip of Marion's tongue.

Lilli's expression clouded with confusion, but she could read her mother's loud and clear, and began walking back towards the house.

Marion watched her go. Measured the increasing distance between them in footsteps, and in stalks of dry grass. In heads of grain so heavy with ripeness that they bowed under their own weight, drooping like sick things ready to give up on life.

Maybe I shall run, she thought. *Run in the opposite direction. For miles and miles of never-ending field. Run until I disappear behind the horizon. And she will never even know I have gone.*

With bleak reluctance weighing down her feet, Marion followed her daughter back to the house.

* * *

The incident in the field left sharp hooks in Marion's brain. They pricked at her throughout the rest of the day. Who was the bitch that wore her mother's hat? How dare they trespass on her land?

It couldn't have been her mother's hat. Certainly not her hatpin. The woman was buried with it. Marion remembered seeing it in the coffin.

Ingrid had picked out the clothes to dress the body. A cheek of a thing to do, Marion thought, but she'd been relieved to find most things taken care of when she arrived before the funeral. The paperwork on its own had been exhausting enough. She was shocked to learn she was still in her mother's will. Both a blessing and a curse, she'd said, that the house was left to her.

She couldn't wait to be rid of it.

Lilli spent the rest of the afternoon in the same armchair, glued to her tablet. She looked like a formless lump in her black hoodie. The insipid theme tunes were a screeching chalkboard to Marion's frayed nerves.

She escaped the house, determined to weed the patchy vegetable garden around the back.

Why her mother bothered with garden vegetables on top of cereal crops, she'd never understood. Perhaps it was another false symbol, designed to telegraph a misplaced pride in living off the land.

Marion saw nothing to be proud of. Several tonnes of every harvest would be wasted as surplus. More than half the grains would only go to animal feed. And whatever crop was good enough quality to make it into real food would still likely see its lifetime end in a bin. Bread left to go mouldy on kitchen counters. Supermarket sandwiches rotting in dumpsters. Marion's nose wrinkled at the thought.

The overgrown garden only underlined this. Marion had purposely left it off the property listing – too hopelessly ugly for real estate photos. What could have been a large, pleasant lawn was instead a utilitarian gravel path which demarcated a dozen rectangular beds, lined with decaying wooden borders. Each bed sported a tangle of tall vegetation: leaves pockmarked by snails and stalks black with aphids.

Marion swapped into dungarees and flat ankle boots, and began with the dandelions infesting the gravel. It felt good to tear something up. She pinched the bottom of the stems and pulled them out, roots and all. She threw the plant carcasses in a bucket, to be added to the mammoth compost heap at the bottom of the garden.

She could smell it from here. The wet, musty odour of fetid earth. The smell alone made her feel slimy. She wished she'd worn gloves to pull up the dandelions. The dirt worked deep under her fingernails.

She swiped an arm across her forehead. Despite

clouds in the sky, muggy heat still permeated the air. Marion felt it was making her woozy. One last fistful of weeds, then she'd go back inside.

The last plant was stubborn. Its roots were anchored deep under the gravel. Marion dug her nails in viciously, seeking to scrape away its hold on the earth. Instead, her fingertips sank into something moist.

Horrified, still pinching at the dandelion roots, Marion felt her fingers sucked downwards. The soil turned glutinous under her touch. Oily friction wriggled against her skin, like she'd invaded a nest of mating slugs. She flexed her fingers and made to pull her arm back.

Instead, the soil fell away under her fingers and the sucking earth *tugged* her whole hand into the cavity. Gravel rasped her skin on the way down. Marion yelped, tried to wrench herself free with her other hand while slimy shapes dragged across her buried palm. They left cold trails over her flesh, sending sickly shivers up her forearm where she yanked and yanked.

The shivers moved up her shoulder and across to her chest, filling her lungs with quivering ice. Her whole body shook, muscles spasming, out of control. All the while her hand sank deeper, wet earth closing over her wrist, sucking her in to her elbow. Marion screamed, cursing blindly. She slammed her other hand down as an anchor. Strained against the invisible force dragging her underground.

'Mum?' said a quiet voice behind her.

Whatever spell she was caught in, broke. Marion's hand came free with a fistful of dandelion roots, and a brief patter of soil hitting the ground.

Marion turned bulging eyes to her daughter. '*What?*'

'I want sausages for dinner.'

Marion's nostrils flared, inhaling shuddering lungfuls of air. 'Go inside.'

She stared at the gravel for several minutes. There was no hole where her arm had been. There was no soil on her skin. No slime. Just the dirt caked under her nails.

She fled the garden. Spent what felt like hours scrubbing her hands under a running tap. Breathing fast and shallow as she watched the water cleanse her skin.

The antiquated pipes clanged under the

pressure. It reverberated around the house and followed Marion downstairs to the kitchen. What had inspired the nightmare vision? Maybe the house knew she hated it. Knew she didn't belong there.

Marion fried sausages in a trance; slopped potato and onions onto white plates.

She ate at the head of the vintage dining table, where her mother used to sit. Lilli took the place setting to the side, an awkward right angle separating them.

Marion poured a glass of red wine, sipped it with trembling fingers.

Lilli poked sluggishly at the food on her plate. Silent, as usual.

'How was your day?' Marion asked.

Lilli shrugged. Eyes down.

'How was your *day?*' Marion repeated. Wine sloshed in the glass.

A small mumble. Barely audible. So typical of every interaction. Marion heard the tell-tale flicking of Lilli's fingers under the table.

'Stop that,' she said.

Lilli stirred her potatoes with a limp wrist and

a vacant expression. The other hand still hidden below.

Flick. Flick. Flick.

'*Stop that.*'

Marion's knuckles banged down on the table. Lilli flinched into her hoodie. Fork and food splattered over the wood where she had dropped it with a clatter.

Marion glared at her recoiling form, a little shape lost in a heap of fabric. Above the sound of her own grinding teeth she could still hear her daughter's stimming, muffled as she held both hands between her legs.

It only deepened Marion's dark well of ire.

She gulped a large mouthful of wine. It was sharp. Nearly bitter, as it slithered down her throat.

'Eat your food,' Marion croaked. She watched with hard eyes as Lilli fumbled the fork, falteringly nibbled a piece of onion.

Marion's lip curled as she regarded her own plate. Such bland food that she cooked now. She thought she'd left this lacklustre palate behind when she'd escaped her mother's clutches.

Absconding to the city revealed new realms of experience. She had freedom. Access to the super-market spice aisle. Street-food on every corner of the city. She was surrounded by flavours from continents she'd never conceived of. She fell in love with all of it, the tang of Korean kimchi, the aromatic heat of an Indian bhuna; even the heavy grease and doughy goodness of a not-exactly-Italian pizza at the end of a night out. She bounced from cuisine to cuisine, a gastronomic chameleon forever changing her colours.

But these days there were no spices in her cup-boards. No adventures in her recipe books. No loud music or harsh fabrics in her house. Her fa-vourite woollen blanket, deemed too scratchy; the radio too incessant and confusing. Dim lights and quiet talking, all the time. No overstimulation. All these trade-offs in the name of motherhood.

When was the last time she had even played with Lilli? At least when she was a baby there had been hormones and cute photographs – life buoys to keep them both afloat on the early, stormy tides of maternal experience. But now those memories were fuzzy, the smiling babe turned into a blank stone, and all Marion felt was the way it weighed her down.

When had it all changed?

'You know,' she began, not even sure Lilli was listening, 'in the old days people would say kids like you had been swapped with a changeling child.'

Lilli made no indication that she'd heard. The fork returned to the plate, accompanied by a slow-chewing and the ever-present flick, flick, flick under the table.

Marion swirled her glass. She felt as empty as Lilli looked. 'They'd say it was a trick of pixies, or somesuch. One day a mum would look at her baby and say, "This isn't mine. My child used to smile and laugh. It was such a sweet thing." So it must be an imposter.' She searched for eye contact under her daughter's messy fringe. Received none. 'Are you an imposter, Lilli?'

The girl didn't answer. But the flicking intensified.

Regret coiled in her gut like a restless worm. Marion pushed her plate away with a rattle. 'I'm going to bed. At least put your plate in the sink when you've finished.'

The upstairs lights fizzed when she turned them on.

This is not Lilli's fault, she repeated as she climbed the creaking stairs. *It's Karl's fault. For walking out on us.*

For not taking Lilli with him.

He'd always been Lilli's favourite. He understood her more than Marion could ever hope to manage. All the changes in their house had been his, while Marion watched from the side lines. He was always so much more willing to bend. So much more able.

And yet, that was why he'd left, wasn't it? Because he was sick of bending. Because something broke.

Marion drained her wine in front of the mirror. Took down her bun of hair, then retied it again. The dark rings under her eyes were at odds with her age. She missed the parties, the wild nights. The exotic restaurants and the interesting conversation. Instead she had this dying house and anxiety medication.

She popped her sertraline pill for the day. It was always best with a glass of wine. Made her drowsy. Easier to fall asleep when the headache kicked in.

She dropped onto the shabby single bed. It was a guest room, across the hall from her mother's. The walls were painted an eye-watering yellow. Orange sunlight still filtered through the curtains, turning up their vibrancy and radiating spikes of discomfort into her skull. Marion turned her face into the pillow so she wouldn't have to tolerate it any more.

The wine sat uneasily in her stomach. Bubbling away in her intestines. Maybe the room was spinning. If she buried deep into bed sheets then it wouldn't matter. They smelled of musty cotton.

Marion welcomed the creeping presence of sleep. Where she had permission to be void, to no longer exist for a few hours. Where self-loathing couldn't reach her. On the other side of oblivion.

It was her natural state, she felt.

Some time, long ago, perhaps there had been a real Marion. A girl before the woman, who had known what she wanted and felt all the things she was supposed to feel for all the right reasons. Was it before or after she'd run away from her mother?

Karl had felt like an answer. A path to finding

herself again. Karl, and the dazzling lights of Hamburg, and the small flat they shared . . . until it became too small for three people. Or for two whole people, and one hollow.

Let me be nothing, Marion sighed on the edge of sleep. *So I don't have to pretend to be more.*

As unconsciousness loomed, an invasive aura twitched her mind awake. First, the smell of wet leaf mulch. Then something like burning tar. Was the window open?

She thought of the compost heap in the garden. The silent chemical factory, breaking down matter into its constituent parts. Eating away at organic life until only nitrogen and phosphorous were left.

She thought, madly, that she could hear it breathing, like a living thing. Squelching around the garden, gorging on the ugly beds of cabbages and tubers. Leaving trails of weeds in its wake, spurred into accelerated growth. Ripping up the gravel as it advanced towards the house.

Marion's fingers curled beneath her pillow. Her breathing stuttered.

There was another sound, like footsteps. A crying baby, somewhere in the far distance. Then that potent stench of hot tar. Sticking to the roof of her mouth. Filling her lungs up with fire.

Something was creeping inside the bedsheets. Something reedy, thread-like. Delicate little vines, snaking over her legs. Knotting around her fingers. They reached for her mouth and she inhaled–

'*No!*'

Marion bolted upright, shaking violently and drenched in cold sweat. A dream. A nightmare. She grabbed for her box of sertraline and threw the tablets at the wall. Bastard things. It was the pills. Or this house. Or living with Lilli. She couldn't take it any more.

Slowly, her hammering heart wound down. The room was dark.

She pulled her knees to her chest, and stared at the walls until morning.

* * *

The morning dawned in washed out shades of grey. Marion woke from a fitful doze, groggy and suffering with a thrumming headache.

She moved about the house like a zombie, washed and dressed in a haze. Tramped downstairs in sweatpants and a tank top. Her skin crawled with discomfort, simultaneously cold-clammy from moisture in the air and too sticky-warm for sleeves.

In the dining room, she stared at the dinner plates on the table. Flies buzzed around the food left out to congeal overnight. Stupid girl. Why hadn't she put them in the sink?

'Lilli!' she shouted up the stairs. 'Time to get up!'

She chewed her lip, waiting for a response. A pang of remorse for the words she'd said yesterday found its way onto her tongue. 'I'm going to make pancakes for breakfast. They'll be waiting for you. Whenever you're ready.'

She tidied up the table, cleaned the plates. In the echoing kitchen, grappled with faulty gas rings on the behemoth black range, until one finally clicked and flared into life. Cracked eggs, mixed milk and flour. Poured into a hefty iron frying pan. Waited. Flipped. Waited. Slipped golden discs onto white plates, and garnished with sugar and lemon. And waited.

And waited.

Water dripped from the corroding copper tap over the sink. The pipes gurgled at odd intervals, with dissonant sounds that rebounded off the tiles and stretched into discordant echoes. Slowly, Marion's resolve unwound.

She chewed through her own pancakes with dead-eyed resentment. The lemon was too sour.

When more than an hour had passed and Lilli still hadn't shown her face, Marion picked up her daughter's plate and tipped the food into the bin.

She stamped around the ground floor, simulating her tasks without really doing. Dropped a whole stack of china into a cardboard box, didn't care that it smashed nearly every piece. Found a sack truck to lift one end of the infernal walnut sideboard, managed to lever it, pivoted slightly, screeching as if from the mouths of all three twisted faces as it gouged deep marks across the floor. She left it like that, askew in the middle of the dining room.

In the garden, she grabbed a hoe and raked at the gravel. Weeds and stones and soil, she dragged it all to the edges, fighting tears as she took out her fury on these meaningless things. Feigning productivity, in the same way she feigned compassion, feigned comfort, like the poor imitation she was.

Eventually, the rage drained out of her. She was empty again, nearly pleasantly numb, and ready to face her daughter.

She climbed the stairs with light footsteps. Plastered a smile on her face as she knocked on Lilli's door.

'Lilli, love,' she called in sing-song. 'Time to get up, please.'

No answer. Marion tucked a loose hair behind her ear; untied her bun and retied it. 'Lilli, *love,*' she repeated with more bite between her teeth. 'Get. Up.'

She turned the handle. The door stuck in the frame, warped by the damp air. Marion put her shoulder into it, gave a forceful shove until it came free.

She stumbled into the room. These walls were mint green, embossed with snaking vines in peeling wallpaper. Lilli's bed was unmade, unoccupied. The tablet lay abandoned on top of the covers.

'Lilli?' Marion asked uncertainly.

She checked under the bed and inside the

wardrobe. A breeze tickled her neck like a warm breath, carrying the scent of asphalt to her nose. She turned to the window, where one curtain was untidily swept to the side, caught around the tie back.

Something black and sticky coated the windowsill.

Marion inched forward. The black substance looked fluid, but viscous. A long drip seeped ponderously onto the bare floorboards.

The window was open a crack. Beyond, the fields shone golden in a fleeting ray of morning sun.

A person stood in the field.

Marion pressed her hands to the window, craned her neck. It wasn't Lilli.

The figure in the broad-brimmed hat looked up. Stared right at Marion.

It stretched out its arms, uncurled its fingers. They seemed to flicker in the air like flames. Or maybe like writhing vines. The wheat rustled in the wind; a hostile sound.

The Rye Aunt shall take you away if you do not behave, her mother's voice spat in her head. *She takes all the bad girls. So, be good! Else you'll become the Rye Aunt's child instead.*

And I shall be glad to be rid of you.

Marion couldn't breathe. She was pinned by the stare of the monster in the field. Did she imagine the terrifying whites of those eyes under the shadow of the hat?

She tore away from the window, panting for breath. 'Lilli,' she wheezed. Then shouted, running through the entire house. '*Lilli!*'

The bedrooms were vacant; the bathroom filled with nothing but stains on the old cracked tiles and drips in the limescale-encrusted basin. The copper pipes clanged a rhythm that matched the thumping inside her head, followed her all the way downstairs. In the dining room the walnut dresser laughed at her from all its gaping mouths.

'*Lilli!*'

She was alone in the house. No other bodies on its grounds.

Marion collapsed against the front door, clutching at the handle with white knuckles. She did not want to go outside. Where the Rye Aunt waited.

'I didn't mean it,' she whispered. 'I didn't mean you should take her away.'

Yes, you did, her traitorous conscience murmured. *How long you wished to be free of her. Free of the wretched luck of this child, this accidental pregnancy. Free of this dull life she trapped you in.*

The truth made her hard, like stone. It lived always in the back of her mind, leeching her emotions away. It was so much easier to feel nothing, to avoid sinking into the deep craters of resentment that filled her core like bubbling tar traps. She was a small animal at risk of falling into the sticky pit, a fragile feathered thing without the strength to pull free. Better to be a stone, that couldn't be caught and suffocated.

In the depths of her heart, she knew she had never been a good girl.

She opened the door.

The shining field stretched before her. The Rye Aunt stood motionless in the centre.

Marion urged her legs forward. 'Where is she?' she demanded, striding to the field boundary. The susurrations of the wheat stalks filled her ears. *'Where's Lilli?'*

There was no answer, no sign of understanding. The hat tipped down.

Marion stepped over the field line.

All at once, sound stopped. Marion stumbled, caught off-balance by the change. She spun in a circle, observed the wind still rolling waves across the field. Her own footsteps confounded her, meeting the earth with dead silence instead of the expected squish of mud.

She retrained her sight on the Rye Aunt. Pushed through dry stems that should have crackled under her advance. 'Where is she?' she repeated, her own voice ballooning into the cavities inside her head. 'Where is my daughter?'

Closer now, she made out loose, dusty clothes on the Rye Aunt's figure. Lank hair lifted in the breeze. Turned the colour of old straw. The hat flapped limply.

Marion approached on trembling tiptoes. Looked up into a wooden pole, speared through the middle of an old boiler suit and topped with a wide hat that was tied on with string.

A small, mad laugh escaped her throat. 'A scarecrow.' The thing was only a scarecrow. Slowly, the sounds of the world oozed back in.

Marion turned back towards the house.

She blinked, shook her head. Pulled down her bun and retied it. Looked again. Turned in a slow circle.

'Where is it?' she croaked. Her mouth was dry, parched for water.

Golden wheat stretched for miles in every direction. Miles and miles, until it hit the grey horizon, heavy with rainclouds.

A muffled, mewling sound dragged her eyes back to the scarecrow. Had its arms been folded across its chest before? Where a fat cloth bundle now wriggled in the cradling hold of its hollow limbs.

Marion felt herself pulled toward the bundle. A weak, desperate cry emanated from it. A baby's cry.

She stood under the shadow of the broad hat and twitched back the fold of cloth. Dazzling blue eyes gawked up at her. A wisp of mousy-brown hair curled against the creature's forehead. It blew a bubble from between its lips, momentarily stunned to a hush.

Marion carefully lifted down the infant parcel.

Cradled it in her arms. It was warm against her beating heart.

'What are you doing out here?' she whispered, searching the brilliant depths of its eyes. They seemed to sparkle, even in the dull pre-storm light. Whole galaxies lived in there. A world beyond her reach. She stretched her thumb to stroke its perfect cheek.

The child looked away. Past her, through her. The connection was lost.

The eyes crinkled. Its gummy mouth opened wide and began to scream.

'Stop this,' Marion said fearfully. She tried to stroke its face again. The monster turned its cheek away and wailed louder. *'Stop this!'*

It squirmed in her grasp. Became animal. The bawling noises were sharp pricks to Marion's brain, pricking, pricking, like a butterfly pin. Demonic in their cadences, unrelenting in their wanting. Surely no child made a sound like that. Was this a real child? Was she a real mother?

She longed to hurl the writhing bundle to the ground, bury it under the earth where the sound could no longer reach her.

She thrust it at the scarecrow instead. 'Take it

back!' Marion pleaded. Tears pricked at her eyes. 'Please take it away from me.'

A cold breeze flapped the empty clothes around their pole. In Marion's outstretched arms the weight of the baby crumpled suddenly. She gasped, lurched to catch what seemed to be a falling mass, and landed on her knees with a handful of empty rags.

The cloth dropped in shreds between her fingers. She pawed at the tatters on the ground, raked through them with her fingernails. Searching for the child. It was not there.

A sob bubbled in her throat like tar bubbling from a well. Dark and ugly.

The creaking of a wooden pole alerted her to the scarecrow. She glanced up; found its post empty. A shadow moved on her periphery.

Marion leapt to her feet and ran.

As she raced for the grey horizon, the wheat began to swallow her. Normally chest-high, now it grew past her shoulders, tickled her neck, her face – closed all the way over her head. She was eight years old, running from her mother. From the belt and the cruel words. Most of all from that blue butterfly hatpin. That pin that pricked such fine points into her skin when she misbehaved. Points too fine for anyone to notice. Leaving bruises as delicate as butterflies down her spine.

All Marion had ever been able to do was run.

She stopped, nearly tripped over her own feet as she skidded to a halt. The rustling field laughed at her. Dragged mocking fingers of wheat over her flesh. Marion's fingers curled.

'*It's you, isn't it?*' She screamed at the dirt. 'Are you back from the dead to torment me? *Will I ever be rid of you?*'

She grabbed a fistful of wheat ears and yanked. They tore with a satisfying crunch.

Marion heaved deep breaths. The hairs on the back of her neck prickled. A voice behind her muttered, 'Stupid girl.'

Her mother's voice.

Marion's limbs locked. In her ears she heard the *slap, slap, slap* of the belt in her mother's hand.

There was another sound, too. Familiar. Quiet. *Flick, flick, flick.*

Marion rotated slowly on her heel.

There was Lilli. White-faced and quaking

wildly. Fingers flicking. A pale ghost in the golden sea.

Behind her, an ugly shadow.

The Rye Aunt towered several feet over the girl. A cloud of asphalt-tang sullied the air.

Its spindly fingers rested on her shoulders. Their flesh was gnarled, like skinny tubers. The clothes it wore were indistinct, shifting like a migraine aura from one moment to the next. Briefly they were her mother's working dungarees; then the shape of a dressing gown she wore around the house. Then they were Marion's own clothes, tank top and joggers concealed under layers of shadow.

Marion searched for the butterfly pin.

'Mum,' Lilli squeaked.

Marion tore her eyes away. Saw her daughter fully. Terrified. Eyes begging her to see. To be seen.

The Rye Aunt smiled. It revealed yellow teeth, dripped brown spittle. One hand moved into the folds of its shirt, lifted out a leathery, walnut-stained breast, streaked with lines of tar. The awful fluid leaked from a dark nipple, oozing like treacle.

The monster gripped Lilli's neck with one

hand, and with the other pushed its grotesque bosom towards her mouth.

'Let her go!' Marion screamed. Her voice was a child's. Scared and pathetic.

The Rye Aunt inclined its head to her. Still smiling.

Marion searched her daughter's face. Lilli's eyes skittered everywhere, unable to hold a fixed gaze. Where did the child go? Was it Lilli who had disappeared, or Marion? In how many small ways had she abandoned her daughter? How many ways she had failed and failed, every day.

This is my child, she finally understood. *This is my child and I am her mother.*

Marion raised her chin to the Rye Aunt. Called up the Bad Girl. The Girl Who Talked Back. The Girl Who Ran Away.

'It's me you want,' she declared. 'I deserve to be here. Lilli doesn't. She doesn't deserve any part of this. Let her go.' Marion opened her arms, stared into the darkness under the Rye Aunt's hat. 'Take me, instead.'

I can do this one thing, she pleaded. *Let me do this one right thing.*

The Rye Aunt's hands dropped away from Lilli's shoulders. The girl staggered backwards.

Marion locked eyes with her, mouthed a single word. '*Run.*'

She watched her daughter flee the field. All the way to the boundary Lilli ran, leapt over it onto the dirt track in front of the house. That deceitful house that ensnared them all. She hoped Lilli would run away from it, too. Leave it all behind.

She nearly smiled as Lilli gave a last glance her way. Then the girl sprinted down the road, towards their neighbour's house. She would be all right. She would be all right.

The Rye Aunt reached Marion, wreathed in the overpowering stench of tarmac. Marion convulsed with the urge to vomit. Plant roots snatched at her face and pulled her head back, to behold the Rye Aunt looming over her.

The demon cupped its fat breast and tipped it towards Marion's mouth. The smell clogged her nose. On her spine she felt the pricking of a butterfly hat pin. She wanted to scream, to protest, *I'm a good girl, I'm a good girl.*

Vines twisted around the back of her neck,

holding her in place. Marion squeezed her eyes closed. The tar-soaked nipple forced into her mouth. Pumped boiling sludge down her throat. She burned from the inside out. Suckled like a monstrous child, unmade, un-personed, unburdened of everything that tortured her. She sank into the deep tar traps within her soul and let go.

Plant tendrils coiled around her limbs. Stretched her skin taut. Dragged her down into the earth. Soil closed over her head, still caught in the Rye Aunt's iron embrace.

The wheat fields glimmered gold and full in the dying afternoon light.

In everlasting darkness beneath them, Marion repeated:

I am a good girl. I am a good girl.

About the Author

Georgina Jeffery is a British author of speculative fiction. Her stories often blend elements of fantasy, humour, and horror, and tend to reflect her fascination with folklore from around the world. You'll find mythical beasties, malevolent spirits, and eldritch magic in a lot of her writing.

Georgina's work can be found in a variety of anthologies and journals, including *The NoSleep Podcast, Sci-Fi Lampoon, Unbreakable Ink, The San Cicaro Experience,* and *Copperfield Review Quarterly.*

ALSO BY GEORGINA JEFFERY

The Jack Hansard Series: Season One

Funny urban fantasy with a lot of British folklore. Jack Hansard, occult salesman, turns reluctant detective when his merchandise is stolen and becomes embroiled in a supernatural kidnapping case.

The Jack Hansard Series: Season Two

Jack Hansard and his coblyn friend Ang are back in business. Together they face shapeshifters, piskies, and ancient magics in their quest to track down Ang's missing kin and uncover the secrets of Baines & Grayle.

Beyond Thundering Waters (Dark Folklore)

A dark fairy tale in a modern Norwegian setting. When a young girl meets a huldra in the Norwegian wilderness, she unwittingly makes a supernatural bargain that puts her Pappa's life at stake.

Within Trembling Caverns (Dark Folklore)

A dark fairy tale in a modern Polish setting. A grandmother cares for an ailing dragon . . . but her compassion places her own family in the jaws of danger.

Across Screaming Seas (Dark Folklore)

A dark fairy tale in a modern Welsh setting. A diver finds herself trapped in a mermaid's lair, wrestling against her own conscience and the need to survive.

The Hub

A supernatural short story with a sci-fi edge. When an app developer accidentally creates a maliciously benevolent social media network, only her girlfriend can save her from what she's brought to life